안도현 시선

안도현
시선

Poems by Ahn Do-Hyun

안선재 옮김

Translated by Brother Anthony of Taizé

POET

아시아

차례
Contents

안도현
시선
Poems by Ahn Do-Hyun

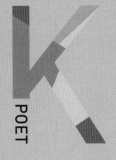

POET

청진 여자

내가 사는 남쪽 나라

쓸쓸한 눈 내리면,

미군 없는 청진항에서

헌 자전거 한 대 빌어 타고

퍼붓는 눈발을 따라가서

어둠을 털어내는 전등을 밝힌 집

백설기 같은 김이 하얗게 서린

유리문 열고 들어서면

갈탄 난로가 뜨거운 집

이름도 버리고 돈도 없이 왔노라고

내가 등 푸른 한 마리 정어리로

당신과 헤엄치고 싶다 말하면

동해 같은 자궁을 열어주는

사랑이라는 말보다 더 아름다운

청진 여자, 그녀와 하룻밤 자고 싶다

봄에 눈이 온다는

Woman of Cheongjin

In the southern land where I live,

when sad snow falls,

in Cheongjin Harbor with no GIs around,

borrowing an old bicycle

and following the thickly falling snow flurries,

where a house turns on lights that expel the gloom,

opening the glass door steamed over white like white rice cake

and going inside, a house with a hot lignite stove burning,

as I say: "I have come; I have given up my name; I bring no money;

I want to swim with you like a blue-backed sardine,"

as she opens a womb like the East Sea,

more beautiful than the word 'love,'

I want to spend a night sleeping with her, that woman of Cheongjin.

Somewhere near Cheongjin Harbor with its clear water

물 맑은 청진항 부근에서

꿈의 벌레 같은 눈송이들이

이부자리를 따뜻하게 적시는 밤

아내를 남쪽에 두고

나는 죄짓는 마음도 모르고

헝클어진 머리카락 미역냄새를 맡으면

부끄럼없이 굵어지는 어깨와 팔뚝

한반도의 허리를 꼭 껴안듯이

더 깊은 신천지 속으로

힘차게 나를 밀어 넣으면

온 바다로 파도 치는

청진 여자, 그녀와 하룻밤 자고 싶다

내가 사는 남쪽 나라

쓸쓸한 눈 내리면,

모든 것을 다 주어야

비로소 하나 되는 날

그 설레이는 첫새벽에

동해 붉은 해 같은 아이를 낳아

넘치는 젖을 물리게 될 청진 여자여,

where it's said it snows in springtime,

one night, as snowflakes like dream insects

warmly soak the bedding,

leaving my wife down south,

with no sense of committing a sin,

as I sniff the seaweed scent of tangled hair,

as I force myself

into a deeper new world

embracing without shame

the angular shoulders and arms

and waist of the Korean peninsula

I want to spend a night sleeping with her, that
woman of Cheongjin,

whose waves break as the whole ocean.

When snow comes falling

on the lonely southern land where I live,

on that day when we finally become one

having given our all,

in that throbbing early dawn,

after giving birth to a babe like the red sun of the
East Sea,

woman of Cheongjin, you will give suck with over-
flowing milk,

우리는 간섭받지 않는

부부가 되고 싶다.

for we want to become parents

free of all interference.

그대에게 가고 싶다

해 뜨는 아침에는
나도 맑은 사람이 되어
그대에게 가고 싶다
그대 보고 싶은 마음 때문에
밤새 퍼부어대던 눈발이 그치고
오늘은 하늘도 맨 처음인 듯 열리는 날
나도 금방 헹구어낸 햇살이 되어
그대에게 가고 싶다
그대 창가에 오랜만에 볕이 들거든
긴 밤 어둠 속에서 캄캄하게 띄워 보낸
내 그리움으로
사랑에 빠진 사람보다 더 행복한 사람은
그리움 하나로 무장무장
가슴이 타는 사람 아니냐

진정 내가 그대를 생각하는 만큼
새날이 밝아오고

I Long to Go Toward You

In the morning, as the sun rises,
I become an innocent fellow
and long to go to you.
On account of a heart longing to see you
the snow that was driving down all night long stops.
Today is a day when the sky opens as though for
the first time.
I become the newly rinsed sunlight
and long to go toward you.
If light shines on your window at long last,
by my yearning
that has floated black in the long night's dark
someone happier than a person in love
is one whose heart is fiercely blazing
with one single yearning, surely?

If the new day dawns
as much as truly I think of you,
if this world can become as beautiful
as truly I come closer to you,

진정 내가 그대 가까이 다가가는 만큼
이 세상이 아름다워질 수 있다면
그리하여 마침내 그대와 내가
하나되어 우리라고 이름 부를 수 있는
그날이 온다면
봄이 올 때까지는 저 들에 쌓인 눈이
우리를 덮어줄 따뜻한 이불이라는 것도
나는 잊지 않으리

사랑이란
또 다른 길을 찾아 두리번거리지 않고
그리고 혼자서는 가지 않는 것
지치고 상처입고 구멍난 삶을 데리고
그대에게 가고 싶다
우리가 함께 만들어야 할 신천지
우리가 더불어 세워야 할 나라
사시사철 푸른 풀밭으로 불러다오
나도 한 마리 튼튼하고 착한 양이 되어
그대에게 가고 싶다

if that day is dawning

when finally you and I, becoming one,

can call ourselves 'we,'

then I will not forget

summoning the snow piled up on the fields,

a warm quilt to cover us.

Love being a matter

of not glancing around or taking another path,

of not advancing alone,

I long to go toward you,

bringing a weary, wounded, threadbare life.

The new world we must create together,

the nation we must establish together,

you should call a meadow that is green in every

season.

Turning into a plump, placid sheep,

I long to go toward you.

가을 엽서

한 잎 두 잎 나뭇잎이
낮은 곳으로
자꾸 내려앉습니다
세상에 나누어줄 것이 많다는 듯이

나도 그대에게 무엇을 좀 나눠주고 싶습니다

내가 가진 게 너무 없다 할지라도
그대여
가을 저녁 한때
낙엽이 지거든 물어보십시오
사랑은 왜
낮은 곳에 있는지를

Autumn Postcard

One by one, leaves
keep falling, settling
in lowly places.
They seem to be saying there's plenty to share in life

And I long to share something with you.

I have very little to offer, but still
one autumn evening
as the leaves are falling, I want
you
to ask me why love
is found in lowly places.

우리가 눈발이라면

우리가 눈발이라면

허공에서 쭈빗쭈빗 흩날리는

진눈깨비는 되지 말자

세상이 바람 불고 춥고 어둡다 해도

사람이 사는 마을

가장 낮은 곳으로

따뜻한 함박눈이 되어 내리자

우리가 눈발이라면

잠 못 든 이의 창문가에서는

편지가 되고

그이의 깊고 붉은 상처 위에 돋는

새 살이 되자

If We Are Falling Snow

If we are falling snow,

let us not turn into sleet

that goes drifting sluggish through the air.

Though the world may be dark, the wind blow cold,

let us turn into thick, warm snowflakes and fall

on the lowest places

in villages where people live.

If we are falling snow,

let us turn into messages

at the window of one unable to sleep,

become new flesh

covering that person's deep, crimson wounds.

마지막 편지

내 사는 마을 쪽에
쥐똥 같은 불빛 멀리 가물거리거든
사랑이여
이 밤에도 울지 않으려고 애쓰는
내 마음인 줄 알아라
우리가 세상 어느 모퉁이에서
헤어져 남남으로
한 번도 만나지 않은 듯
서로 다른 길이 되어 가더라도
어둠은 또 이불이 되어
우리를 덮고
슬픔도 가려주리라

그대 진정 나를 사랑하거든
사랑했었다는 그 말은 하지 말라
그대가 뜨락에 혼자 서 있더라도
등 뒤로 지는 잎들을

Last Letter

In the direction of the village where I live
a tiny light glimmers in the distance.
Ah, my love!
Understand that it's my heart
striving not to cry tonight.
Parting at some corner of this world, estranged,
as if we had never met,
we go our separate ways,
yet once darkness becomes our quilt
and covers us
it covers our sorrow too.

If truly you love me,
do not say that you loved me.
Though you stand alone in the garden,
do not show me the leaves falling behind your back;
if on nights when you cannot sleep
the windows of your lonely house rattle,
do not think
it's the sound of me knocking

내게 보여주지는 말고
잠들지 못하는 밤
그대의 외딴집 창문이 덜컹댄다 해도
행여 내가 바람되어 두드리는 소리로
여기지 말라

모든 것을 내주고도
알 수 없는 그윽한 기쁨에
돌아앉아 몸을 떠는 것이 사랑이라지만
이제 이 세상을 나누어 껴안고
우리는 괴로워하리라
내 마지막 편지가 쓸쓸하게
그대 손에 닿거든
사랑이여
부디 울지 말라
길 잃은 아이처럼 서 있지 말고
그대가 길이 되어 가거라

having turned into wind.

They say that love is a matter of turning one's back
and shuddering
  with an unspeakable, quiet joy,
  after giving everything,
  but now we have shared up this world, each embracing a part,
  and suffer torment.
  If my last letter sadly touches your hand,
  my love,
  don't cry, I beg.
  Do not stand like a child that has lost its way.
  Become your own path and go.

땅

내게 땅이 있다면

거기에 나팔꽃을 심으리

때가 오면

아침부터 저녁까지 보랏빛 나팔소리가

내 귀를 즐겁게 하리

하늘 속으로 덩굴이 애쓰며 손을 내미는 것도

날마다 눈물 젖은 눈으로 바라보리

내게 땅이 있다면

내 아들에게는 한 평도 물려 주지 않으리

다만 나팔꽃이 다 피었다 진 자리에

동그랗게 맺힌 꽃씨를 모아

아직 터지지 않은 세계를 주리

Ground

If I had some ground
I would sow it with morning glories
so that in due time
from morning to night purple trumpet music
would delight my ears.
Every day I would watch with tear-drenched eyes
as tendrils stretched into the sky with all their
might.
If I had some ground
I would not leave my son a single square yard.
Instead, on the spot where the flowers had bloomed
and faded
I would gather together the spherical seeds
and leave him a world that has not yet opened.

이 세상에 아이들이 없다면

어른들도 없을 것이다

어른들이 없으므로 교육도 없을 것이다

교육이 없으므로 교과서도 없을 것이다

교과서가 없으므로 시험도 없을 것이다

시험이 없으므로 대학교도 없을 것이다

대학교가 없으므로 고등학교도 없을 것이다

고등학교가 없으므로 중학교도 없을 것이다

중학교가 없으므로 국민학교도 없을 것이다

국민학교가 없으므로 운동장도 없을 것이다

운동장이 없으므로 미끄럼틀도 없을 것이다

미끄럼틀을 타고

매일 매일 하늘에서 내려오는

눈부신 하느님을 본 사람은 아무도 없을 것이다

If There Were No Children
in the World

There would be no grown-ups, either.

There being no grown-ups, there would be no education.

There being no education, there would be no text books.

There being no text books, there would be no exams.

There being no exams, there would be no universities.

There being no universities, there would be no high schools.

There being no high schools, there would be no middle schools.

There being no middle schools, there would be no primary schools.

There being no primary schools, there would be no playgrounds.

There being no playgrounds, there would be no slides.

There would be nobody who ever saw how, dazzling, God comes sliding down
from heaven every day

제비꽃에 대하여

제비꽃을 알아도 봄은 오고
제비꽃을 몰라도 봄은 간다

제비꽃에 대해 알기 위해서
따로 책을 뒤적여 공부할 필요는 없지

연인과 들길을 걸을 때 잊지 않는다면
발견할 수 있을 거야

그래, 허리를 낮출 줄 아는 사람에게만
보이는 거야 자줏빛이지

자줏빛을 톡 한번 건드려봐
흔들리지? 그건 관심이 있다는 뜻이야

사랑이란 그런 거야
사랑이란 그런 거야

Concerning Violets

Though you know about violets, spring comes;
though you know nothing about violets, spring goes.

In order to find out about violets
there's no need to browse books, studying particu-
larly.

As you walk with a lover along field paths, if you do
not forget
you can discover them.

That's right, they can only be seen by someone
who knows how to bend down low. They're a purple
color.

Try touching the purple once.
You falter? That's a sign of interest.

Love's like that.
Love's like that.

봄은,

제비꽃을 모르는 사람을 기억하지 않지만

제비꽃을 아는 사람 앞으로는

그냥 가는 법이 없단다

그 사람 앞에는

제비꽃 한포기를 피워두고 가거든

참 이상하지?

해마다 잊지 않고 피워두고 가거든

Spring

does not remember anyone who is ignorant about violets

but in the presence of someone who knows about violets

it does not simply go.

Before such a person

it brings a clump of violets into bloom, then goes.

Strange, isn't it?

Every year, not forgetting, bringing into bloom, then going.

바닷가 우체국

바다가 보이는 언덕 위에

우체국이 있다

나는 며칠 동안 그 마을에 머물면서

옛사랑이 살던 집을 두근거리며 쳐다보듯이

오래오래 우체국을 바라보았다

키 작은 측백나무 울타리에 둘러싸인 우체국은

문 앞에 붉은 우체통을 세워두고

하루 내내 흐린 눈을 비비거나 귓밥을 파기 일쑤였다

우체국이 한 마리 늙고 게으른 짐승처럼 보였으나

나는 곧 그 게으름을 이해할 수 있었다

내가 이곳에 오기 아주 오래 전부터

우체국은 아마

두 눈이 짓무르도록 수평선을 바라보았을 것이고

그리하여 귓속에 파도 소리가 모래처럼 쌓였을 것이

었다

나는 세월에 대하여 말하지만 결코

세월을 큰 소리로 탓하지는 않으리라

Seaside Post Office

On a hill overlooking the sea

there is a post office.

When I stayed in that village for a few days

I gazed at the post office for a long time,

as if looking with beating heart at the house of a
former sweetheart.

Surrounded by a low thuja-tree fence, the post office

had a red mailbox set in front of the door

and all day long I kept rubbing my dim eyes or dig-
ging at my ears.

The post office looked like an old, lazy animal

but I could understand that laziness.

Long before I came here

the post office had probably

been gazing at the horizon until its eyes were sore,

while the sound of waves must have piled up like
sand in its ears.

I talk about time but

I would never blame time in a loud voice.

한번은 엽서를 부치러 우체국에 갔다가

줄지어 소풍 가는 유치원 아이들을 만난 적이 있다

내 어린 시절에 그랬던 것처럼

우체통이 빨갛게 달아오른 능금 같다고 생각하거나

편지를 받아먹는 도깨비라고

생각하는 소년이 있을지도 모르는 일이었다

그러다가 소년의 코밑에 수염이 거뭇거뭇 돋을 때쯤
이면

우체통에 대한 상상력은 끝나리라

부치지 못한 편지를

가슴속 주머니에 넣어두는 날도 있을 것이며

오지 않는 편지를 혼자 기다리는 날이 많아질 뿐

사랑은 열망의 반대쪽에 있는 그림자 같은 것

그런 생각을 하다 보면

삶이 때로 까닭도 없이 서러워진다

우체국에서 편지 한 장 써보지 않고

인생을 다 안다고 말하는 사람들을 또 길에서 만난다
면

나는 편지봉투의 귀퉁이처럼 슬퍼질 것이다

바다가 문 닫을 시간이 되어 쓸쓸해지는 저물녘

Once, when I went to the post office to send off a postcard,

I met a line of kindergarten kids going for a picnic.

Perhaps there might have been a boy

thinking that the mailbox looked like a red-hot crab apple

or a goblin ready to eat the letters,

as I did in my childhood.

Then, by the time a beard has grown thick beneath the boy's nose

he will have ceased imagining things about mailboxes.

There will be days when he stows away in a pocket in his heart

a letter he could not send

and there will be more days when he waits alone for a letter that does not come.

When I think about how

love is like a shadow on the far side of desire,

life sometimes grows sorrowful without cause.

If I meet people again on the street who say they know everything about life

without ever writing a single letter in the post office

I grow sad like the corners of an envelope.

퇴근을 서두르는 늙은 우체국장이 못마땅해할지라도

나는 바닷가 우체국에서

만년필로 잉크 냄새 나는 편지를 쓰고 싶어진다

내가 나에게 보내는 긴 편지를 쓰는

소년이 되고 싶어진다

나는 이 세상에 살아남기 위해 사랑을 한 게 아니었다고

나는 사랑을 하기 위해 살았다고

그리하여 한 모금의 따뜻한 국물 같은 시를 그리워하

였고

한 여자보다 한 여자와의 연애를 그리워하였고

그리고 맑고 차가운 술을 그리워하였다고

밤의 염전에서 소금 같은 별들이 쏟아지면

바닷가 우체국이 보이는 여관방 창문에서 나는

느리게 느리게 굴러가다가 머물러야 할 곳이 어디인

가를 아는

우체부의 자전거를 생각하고

이 세상의 모든 길이

우체국을 향해 모였다가

다시 갈래갈래 흩어져 산골짜기로도 가는 것을 생각

하고

As dusk grows sad when the time comes for the sea to close its doors,

even if the old postmaster disapproves, in a hurry to go home,

at the seaside post office

I find myself wanting to write with a fountain pen a letter that smells of ink.

I find myself wanting to be a boy

writing a long letter addressed to myself.

Saying that I did not love in order to survive in this world

but that I lived in order to love,

and that therefore I longed for a poem like warm soup,

that I longed for a love affair with a woman rather than for a woman

and that I longed for clear, cold liquor,

and when salt-like stars pour down on the night-time salt ponds

at the window of the inn room from where the seaside post office is visible

I think about the bicycle the postman rides slowly, slowly,

knowing just where he has to stop;

길은 해변의 벼랑 끝에서 끊기는 게 아니라

훌쩍 먼바다를 건너기도 한다는 것을 생각한다

그리고 때로 외로울 때는

파도 소리를 우표 속에 그려넣거나

수평선을 잡아당겼다가 놓았다가 하면서

나도 바닷가 우체국처럼 천천히 늙어갔으면 좋겠다고

생각한다

and about how all the roads of this world,

after gathering and heading toward the post office,

scatter again, with some heading for mountain val-
leys,

and how the road does not break off at the edge of
the seaside cliffs

but crosses straight across the distant sea.

And sometimes, feeling lonely,

as I draw the sound of the waves on a stamp

or pull on the horizon then let it go again,

I think

how good it would be if I, too, could grow old like
the seaside post office.

고래를 기다리며

고래를 기다리며

나 장생포 바다에 있었지요

누군가 고래는 이제 돌아오지 않는다, 했지요

설혹 돌아온다고 해도 눈에는 보이지 않는다고요,

나는 서러워져서 방파제 끝에 앉아

바다만 바라보았지요

기다리는 것은 오지 않는다는 것을

알면서도 기다리고, 기다리다 지치는 게 삶이라고

알면서도 기다렸지요

고래를 기다리는 동안

해변의 젖꼭지를 빠는 파도를 보았지요

숨을 한 번 내쉴 때마다

어깨를 들썩이는 그 바다가 바로

한 마리 고래일지도 모른다고 생각했지요

Waiting for Whales

There I was beside the sea at Jangsaengpo
waiting for whales.
Somebody told me that whales no longer came visiting nowadays.
Even if they come visiting, they cannot be seen.
Saddened, I sat at the end of the breakwater
and looked out to sea.
Though I knew that what we wait for never comes,
I waited; though I knew that life
is a matter of growing weary of waiting,
I waited.
While I waited, I watched the waves
suck at the seashore's nipples.
I reflected that perhaps the sea
with its shoulders heaving every time it took a
breath
was in fact a whale.

꽃

바깥으로 뻗어내지 않으면 고통스러운 것이
몸 속에 있기 때문에
꽃은, 핀다
솔직히 꽃나무는
꽃을 피워야 한다는 게 괴로운 것이다

내가 너를 그리워하는 것,
이것은 터뜨리지 않으면 곪아 썩는 못난 상처를
바로 너에게 보내는 일이다
꽃이 허공으로 꽃대를 밀어올리듯이

그렇다 꽃대는
꽃을 피우는 일이 너무 힘들어서
자기 몸을 세차게 흔든다
사랑이여, 나는 왜 이렇게 아프지도 않는 것이냐

몸 속의 아픔이 다 말라버리고 나면

A Flower

Because there is something in the body
that hurts if it is not spat out,
a flower, blooms.
Honestly, it is painful
for a flowering plant to have to bloom.

My longing for you,
if it does not burst, will be the same as sending you
a festering, rotting, unsightly wound.
Just as a flower pushes up a stem into the air.

Yes.
It's so hard for a flower stalk to bloom
that it shakes its body fiercely.
Love, why am I not sick like that?

Once all the pain in my body has dried up
I'm afraid my longing, too, will no longer smell sweet.

After I struggled all night long to survive,

내 그리움도 향기나지 않을 것 같아 두렵다

살아남으려고 밤새 발버둥을 치다가

입 안에 가득 고인 피,

뱉을 수도 없고 뱉지 않을 수도 없을 때

꽃은, 핀다

with my mouth full of blood,

that I can neither spit out nor not spit out,

a flower, blooms.

오래된 우물

뒤안에 우물이 딸린 빈집을 하나 얻었다

아, 하고 소리치면
아, 하고 소리를 받아주는
우물 바닥까지 언젠가 한 번은 내려가보리라고
혼자서 상상하던 시절이 있었다
우물의 깊이를 알 수 없었기에 나는 행복하였다

빈집을 수리하는데
어린것들이 빗방울처럼 통통거리며 뛰어다닌다
우물의 깊이를 알고 있기에
나는 슬그머니 불안해지기 시작하였다
오래 된 우물은
땅속의 쓸모없는 허공인 것

나는 그 입구를 아예 막아버리기로 작정하였다
우물을 막고 나서는

The Ancient Well

I took possession of an empty house with a well in
its back yard.

There was a time when I used to imagine myself
going down to the bottom of the well
which when I shouted "Ah!"
would answer back "Ah."
Since there was no knowing the depth of the well, I
was happy.

I repaired the empty house
and the children went pounding and running
around.
Knowing how deep the well was,
I began to feel secretly uneasy.
That ancient well
being a useless hole in the ground

I decided to block its mouth once and for ever.
After the well was covered over

나, 방안에서 안심하고 시를 읽으리라

인부를 불러 메우지 않을 바에야 미룰 것도 없었다

눈꺼풀을 쓸어내리듯 함석으로 덮고

쓰다 만 베니어 합판을 덧씌우고

그 위에다 끙끙대며 돌덩이를 몇 개 얹어 눌렀다

그리하여

우물은 죽었다

우물이 죽었다고 생각하자

나는 갑자기 눈앞이 캄캄해졌다

한때 찰박찰박 두레박이 내려올 때마다

넘치도록 젖을 짜주던 저 우물은

이 집의 어머니,

별똥별이 지는 밤하늘을 밤새도록 올려다보다가

더러는 눈물 글썽이기도 하였을

저 우물은

이 집의 눈동자였는지 모른다

나는 우물의 눈알을 파먹은 몹쓸 인간이 되어

I would be able to read poetry calmly in my room.

I had no reason to delay if I was not going to hire workers to fill it in.

I covered it with a steel sheet as if closing its eyelid

then crowned that with a piece of plywood

and placed a few heavy stones on top of that, grumbling as I did so.

At that,

the well died.

As soon as the thought came to me that the well had died

everything suddenly grew black before me.

Previously, every time I squeakingly let down the bucket

that well had generously provided milk,

it was the house's mother;

it would spend the night gazing up at the sky and its falling stars

and sometimes brim with tears,

as if perhaps the well

were the house's eyes.

소리친다

아, 하고 소리쳐도

아, 하고 소리를 받아주지 않는

우물에다 대고

I, the scoundrel who had put out the well's eyes,

cried out

to the well,

which though I shouted "Ah!"

no longer answered back "Ah!"

해찰

봄날, 병아리가 어미 꽁무니를 쫓아가고 있다
나란히 되똥되똥 줄 맞춰 가고 있다

연둣빛 풀밭은 병아리들 발바닥을 들어올려 주느라
바쁘다
꽃이 진 자리에 꽃씨를 밀어 올리느라 민들레꽃도 바
쁘다

민들레 꽃대 끝에 웬 솜털 같은 눈이 내렸나?
병아리 한 마리 대열에서 이탈해 한눈을 팔고 있다

그리고는 꽃씨에다 노란 부리를 톡, 대어 본다
병아리는 햇빛을 타고 날아간다
허공에다 발자국을 콕콕 찍으며 하늘하늘 날아간다

Brashness

One spring day, chicks are chasing their mother's tail.

Wobbling from side to side they struggle to keep in line.

The bright green grass is kept busy lifting the chicks' feet

and the dandelions are busy pushing up seeds in place of flowers.

Has downy snow fallen on the tips of the dandelion stalks?

One chick has left the line and is looking aside.

Then it touches the seeds with its yellow beak.

The chick goes flying up, borne on the sunlight.

Leaving footprints printed in the air, it goes flying lightly away.

간격

숲을 멀리서 바라보고 있을 때는 몰랐다

나무와 나무가 모여

어깨와 어깨를 대고

숲을 이루는 줄 알았다

나무와 나무 사이

넓거나 좁은 간격이 있다는 걸

생각하지 못했다

벌어질 대로 최대한 벌어진,

한데 붙으면 도저히 안 되는,

기어이 떨어져 서 있어야 하는,

나무와 나무 사이

그 간격과 간격이 모여

鬱鬱蒼蒼 숲을 이룬다는 것을

산불이 휩쓸고 지나간

숲에 들어가 보고서야 알았다

Gaps

I did not realize it when I looked at the forest from
far away.
I thought that
one tree after another had gathered together,
shoulder to shoulder,
and formed a forest.
It never struck me
that between one tree and another
there is a gap, wide or narrow.
They are separated, as far apart as possible;
it would not do for them to be all clustered together.
One tree must stand well apart from the next,
for it's the gaps between them gathered together
that compose a leafy, green forest.
I only realized that after I went into the forest
and looked after a fire had swept through it.

모기장 동물원

나방이 왔다 풍뎅이가 왔다 매미가 왔다
형광등 불빛 따라 와서 모기장 바깥에 붙어 있다
오지 말라고 모기장을 쳐 놓으니까 젠장, 아주 가까이
와서
나를 내려다보며 읽고 있다

영락없이 모기장 동물원에 갇힌
나는 한 마리의 슬픈 포유류

책을 덮고 생각중이다
저 곤충 손님들에게는 내가
모기장 안쪽에 있는가
바깥쪽에 있는가

A Mosquito-Net Zoo

Moths have come. Beetles have come. Cicadas have come.

Attracted by the fluorescent light, they cling to the mosquito net.

I put up the mosquito net to stop them coming, but damn it all,

they have come as close as they can,

they're looking down on me, reading me.

Firmly trapped in a mosquito-net zoo,

I am a sad mammal.

I've put down my book and am thinking.

For those insect visitors,

am I inside the mosquito net?

Or outside?

명자꽃

그해 봄 우리 집 마당가에 핀 명자꽃은 별스럽게도 붉
었습니다

옆집에 살던 명자 누나 때문이라고 나는 생각하였습
니다

나는 누나의 아랫입술이 다른 여자애들보다 도톰한
것을 생각하고는 혼자 뒷방 담요 위에서 명자나무 이파
리처럼 파랗게 뒤척이며

명자꽃을 생각하고 또 문득 누나에게도 낯설었을 初
經이며 누나의 속옷이 받아낸 붉디붉은 꽃잎까지 속속
들이 생각하였습니다

그러다가 꽃잎에 입술을 대보았고 나는 소스라치게
놀랐습니다

내 짝사랑의 어리석은 입술이 칼날처럼 서럽고 차가
운 줄을 처음 알게 된

그해는 4월도 반이나 넘긴 중순에 눈이 내린 까닭이
었습니다

Flowering Myeongja Quince Blossom

In the spring that year, the flowers of the myeongja flowering quince in our garden were exceptionally red.

I thought it was because of Myeongja, the girl who lived next door.

I thought that her lower lip was fuller than those of other girls, as I tossed and turned like a quince leaf, alone on my blanket in my back room,

thinking about quince flowers, and her unaccustomed first period, I even kept thinking of the deep red petals that her underwear had welcomed.

Then I put my lips to those petals and I was amazed, appalled.

That was the first time I knew that the foolish lips of my unrequited love were sad and cold like a knife blade.

It snowed beyond mid-April that year

and as the snowflakes came falling, for the first time running around darting my tongue in and out did not

하늘 속의 눈송이가 내려와서 혀를 날름거리며 달아
나는 일이 애당초 남의 일 같지 않았습니다

명자 누나의 아버지는 일찍 늙은 명자나무처럼 등짝
이 어둡고 먹먹했는데 어쩌다 그 뒷모습만 봐도 벌 받
을 것 같아

나는 스스로 먼저 병을 얻었습니다

나의 낡은 자리에 누워 이마로 찬 수건을 받는 일이었
습니다

어린 나를 관통해서 아프게 한 명자꽃,

그 꽃을 산당화라고 부르기도 한다는 것을 알게 될 무렵

홀연 우리 옆집 명자 누나는 혼자 서울로 떠났습니다

떨어진 꽃잎이 쌓인 명자나무 밑동은 추했고, 봄은 느
긋한 봄이었기에 지루하였습니다

나는 왜 식물도감을 뒤적여야 하는가,

명자나무는 왜 다닥다닥 紅燈을 달았다가 일없이 발
등에 떨어뜨리는가,

내 불평은 꽃잎 지는 소리만큼이나 소소한 것이었지
마는

명자 누나의 소식은 첫 월급으로 자기 엄마한테 빨간
내복 한 벌 사서 보냈다는 풍문이 전부였습니다

seem like something anyone should do.

Myeongja's father's back was dark and stubborn like a prematurely aged quince tree; somehow, simply seeing his back was already a punishment.

So I made myself sick first.

My delight was to lie on my bed and have a cool towel pressed to my forehead.

The myeongja flowers that had pierced my young heart

were also called by other names, I learned, just at the time

when Myeongja abruptly left for Seoul alone.

The roots of the myeongja, covered with fallen petals, were ugly, and the spring was boring because I was idle.

Why did I have to keep studying a book about botany, I wondered?

Why did a myeongja quince display clusters of red lights then, without more ado, drop them on my feet?

My complaint was as slight as the sound of a petal falling.

The only news of Myeongja was a rumor that she had used her first salary to send her mother a set of red underwear.

해마다 내가 개근상을 받듯 명자꽃이 피어도 누나는 돌아오지 않았고,

　　내 눈에는 전에 없던 핏줄이 창궐하였습니다

　　명자 누나네 집의 내 키만 한 창문 틈으로 붉은 울음소리가 새어나오던 저녁이 있었습니다

　　그 울음소리는 自盡할 듯 뜨겁게 쏟아지다가 잦아들고 그러다가는 또 바람벽 치는 소리를 섞으며 밤늦도록 이어졌습니다

　　그 이튿날, 누나가 집에 다녀갔다고, 애비 없는 갓난애를 업고 왔었다고 수런거리는 소리가

　　명자나무 가시에 뾰족하게 걸린 것을 나는 보아야 했습니다

　　잎이 나기 전에 꽃 몽우리를 먼저 뱉는 꽃,

　　그날은 눈이 퉁퉁 붓고 머리가 헝클어진 명자꽃이 그해의 첫 꽃을 피우던 날이었습니다

Although the myeongja quince bloomed every year, as I received the prize for perfect attendance at school, Myeongja never came back

and in my eyes blood raged that had not been there before.

There came an evening when a crimson sound of crying leaked out through the low windows of Myeongja's house.

The crying lasted until late into the night, pouring out hot as if someone wished to put an end to their life, then faded away, then mingled with a sound of walls being struck.

The next day, I was obliged to see hanging sharp on the branches of the quince the sound of chatter about how Myeongja had briefly visited her home, a fatherless child on her back,

buds the flowers spit out before the petals emerge.

That was the day the first myeongja quince flowers of the year blossomed, eyes swollen from weeping, hair dishevelled.

스며드는 것

꽃게가 간장 속에
반쯤 몸을 담그고 엎드려 있다
등판에 간장이 울컥울컥 쏟아질 때
꽃게는 뱃속의 알을 껴안으려고
꿈틀거리다가 더 낮게
더 바닥 쪽으로 웅크렸으리라
버둥거렸으리라 버둥거리다가
어찌 할 수 없어서
살 속으로 스며드는 것을
한때의 어스름을
꽃게는 천천히 받아들였으리라
껍질이 먹먹해지기 전에
가만히 알들에게 말했으리라

저녁이야
불 끄고 잘 시간이야

Permeating

A crab is lying flat,
half-immersed in soy sauce.
When the soy sauce was poured on its back
the crab must have wriggled, crouching ever lower,
ever closer to the bottom,
intent on embracing the eggs in its belly.
It must have squirmed. Then, after squirming,
having no choice,
the crab must slowly have accepted
what was permeating its flesh,
a moment's twilight.
Finally, before the shell grew deaf,
it must quietly have told the eggs:

Evening's come.
Time to turn off the light and go to sleep.

고양이 뼈 한 마리

고양이 뼈 한 마리가 앞다리를 낮추고 바짝 웅크리고 있다

당장에 달아날 듯, 묵은 개나리 가지를 쳐내자, 그 자리에, 바로 뒷발로 땅을 박차고 뛰어오를 듯

고양이 뼈 한 마리가 제 몸을 동그랗게 말고 있다

수염 한 올, 살가죽 한 장 없이, 얼룩무늬도 벗어던지고

이 짐승이 대체 어디를 급히 가려나, 나는 궁금했다

그러다가, 왜, 이곳에, 혼자 와서 숨어 있었는지도 궁금했다

쪼르르 꽃 핀 개나리 가지 같은 꼬리뼈를 한껏 치켜들고 있는 이 고양이 뼈 한 마리는

세상의 소란한 햇빛 따위 작파하고, 약에 취한 듯, 비틀거리듯

쓰러지듯, 이 그늘을 찾아들었을까

세상의 뒤쪽이거나 아래쪽에 기어이 살고 싶었을까

가지런한 갈비뼈로 손수 하얗게 수의를 지어 입은

이 짐승을 찾아, 길을 물어 찾아와, 어느 날 어린것들

One Cat's Bones

The cat's bones are crouching, tense, front legs bent
as if poised for flight, as I began to clear away old
forsythia branches, right there, as if about to kick the
ground with its back legs and make a leap,

The cat's bones are curled up round.

No whiskers, no skin, speckled fur cast off,

I wondered: where was this beast so eager to go?

Then I wondered: why did it come here, all alone, and
hide?

Did these cat bones, tail bone held high like a flowering forsythia branch, abandoning the world's raucous
sunlight and such, visit this shade as if intoxicated,
staggering, collapsing?

Did it simply want to live at the back of the world or
its bottom?

Its children might have come in search of this beast,
now dressed in white, a shroud woven with its own ribs,

searching, asking directions, at times weeping bitterly,
at a loss.

They might have pressed their noses against the

은 떼로 아연 울고불고 하였을 것이고,

　식어버린 이 짐승의 골반에다 코를 대고 한없이 문지
르다가, 문지르다가 돌아갔으리라

　그리하여 이 고양이 뼈 한 마리, 문득 제 뼈를 수습하
다가

　나한테 들킨 게 아니라, 달려 가봐야 한다는 듯

　젖 먹이다가 두고 온 새끼들이 먼데서 앙앙 우는 소리
를 듣고는, 몸을 일으키던 참이었으리라

　몸에 물큰한 젖이 돌아, 견딜 수 없다는 듯, 봄날 저녁에

animal's chill pelvis, rubbed and rubbed, then gone back home.

At which these cat bones might have gathered themselves together,

instead of letting me find them, and on hearing the kittens crying in the distance, the children she had nursed before setting out as if in a rush to go somewhere,

she might have raised herself

as the sweet milk circulated in her body, unable to bear it, one spring evening.

재테크

한 평 남짓 얼 갈이배추 씨를 뿌렸다

스무 날이 지나니 한 뼘 크기의 이파리가 몇 장 펄럭
였다

바람이 이파리를 흔든 게 아니었다, 애벌레들이

제 맘대로 길을 내고 똥을 싸고 길가에 깃발을 꽂는
통에 설핏 펄럭이는 것처럼 보였던 것

동네 노인들이 혀를 차며 약을 좀 하라 했으나

그래야지요, 하고는 그만두었다

한 평 남짓 애벌레를 키우기로 작심했던 것

또 스무 날이 지나 애벌레가 나비가 되면 나는 한 평
얼갈이배추밭의 주인이자 나비의 주인이 되는 것

그리하여 나비는 머지않아 배추밭 둘레의 허공을 다
차지할 것이고

나비가 날아가는 곳까지가, 나비가 울타리를 치고 돌
아오는 그 안쪽까지가

모두 내 소유가 되는 것

Investment Techniques

I sowed cabbage seeds over more than a pyeong of ground.

After twenty days, a few leaves a span high were fluttering.

It was not the wind that shook the leaves. It seemed that caterpillars

had forced open a path, left droppings, fixed flags in cans along the roadside and were making them flutter.

The local elders clacked their tongues and told me to spray them;

I replied that I would do so, and left it at that.

Deciding to grow more than a pyeong of caterpillars,

once the caterpillars became butterflies after another twenty days I would be the owner of a pyeong of cabbage-field and of the butterflies too,

and soon the butterflies would occupy all the air around the cabbage field

so that wherever the butterflies flew, everywhere inside the fence the butterflies erected and flew back from,

would all be mine

일기

오전에 깡마른 국화꽃 웃자란 눈썹을 가위로 잘랐다

오후에는 지난여름 마루 끝에 다녀간 사슴벌레에게
엽서를 써서 보내고

고장 난 감나무를 고쳐주러 온 醫員에게 감나무 그늘
의 수리도 부탁하였다

추녀 끝으로 줄지어 스며드는 기러기 일흔세 마리까
지 세다가 그만두었다

저녁이 부엌으로 사무치게 왔으나 불빛 죽이고 두어
가지 찬에다 밥을 먹었다

그렇다고 해도 이것 말고 무엇이 더 중요하다는 말인가

Diary

In the morning, I cut the scrawny, overgrown eye-brows of chrysanthemum flowers with scissors.

In the afternoon, I wrote and mailed off a postcard to the stag beetle that visited the edge of the porch last summer

I also asked the doctor who came to mend the broken persimmon tree to repair its shade, too.

I counted seventy-three wild geese filing into the edge of the roof, then stopped counting.

The evening penetrated into the kitchen, but I turned down the light and ate from a couple of kinds of cup.

Even so, what can be more important than this?

출처

「청진 여자」: 『모닥불』, 창비, 1989

「그대에게 가고 싶다」: 『그대에게 가고 싶다』, 푸른숲, 2002

「가을 엽서」: 『그대에게 가고 싶다』, 푸른숲, 2002

「우리가 눈발이라면」: 『그대에게 가고 싶다』, 푸른숲, 2002

「마지막 편지」: 『그대에게 가고 싶다』, 푸른숲, 2002

「땅」: 『외롭고 높고 쓸쓸한』, 문학동네, 2004

「이 세상에 아이들이 없다면」: 『외롭고 높고 쓸쓸한』, 문학동네, 2004

「제비꽃에 대하여」: 『그리운 여우』, 창비, 1997

「바닷가 우체국」: 『바닷가 우체국』, 문학동네, 1999

「고래를 기다리며」: 『바닷가 우체국』, 문학동네, 1999

「꽃」: 『바닷가 우체국』, 문학동네, 1999

「오래된 우물」: 『바닷가 우체국』, 문학동네, 1999

「해찰」: 『아무것도 아닌 것에 대하여』, 문학동네, 2005

「간격」: 『너에게 가려고 강을 만들었다』, 창비, 2004

「모기장 동물원」: 『너에게 가려고 강을 만들었다』, 창비, 2004

「명자꽃」: 『간절하게 참 철없이』, 창비, 2008

「스며드는 것」: 『간절하게 참 철없이』, 창비, 2008

「고양이 뼈 한 마리」: 『간절하게 참 철없이』, 창비, 2008

「재테크」: 『북항』, 문학동네, 2012

「일기」: 『북항』, 문학동네, 2012

시인노트
Poet's Note

내가 말에 홀려 살아온 줄 알았는데 그게 아니었다.

내가 쓴 문장이 당신의 마음을 흐리게 만들었다.

당신의 마음을 씻는 일이 결국 내가 해야 할 일인 것
같다.

I thought that I had lived bewitched with words, but it was not so.

The phrases I wrote muddied your heart.

It seems that ultimately it is my task to wash your heart.

해설
Commentary

POET

웅숭깊은 사랑의 공동체

이경수 (문학평론가)

첫 시집 『서울로 가는 전봉준』을 낸 이후 2012년 『북항』을 내고 몇 년간 절필했다 돌아온 최근에 이르기까지, 안도현의 시세계를 관통하는 태도는 소외된 이들을 향한 사랑과 연대의 시선이라고 할 수 있다. 사람들이 모여 사는 세상은 물론 자연을 향해서도 시인의 시선은 낮은 곳, 소외된 곳까지 미친다.

안도현의 시는 사랑이라는 큰 주제 안에 대체로 포괄되는데, 흥미로운 것은 그것이 개인적 사랑의 의미에 머물지 않고 더 넓은 사랑으로 나아간다는 데 있다. 이는 안도현의 시가 1980년대 민중시의 정서를 잇고 있는 점과 깊은 연관을 갖는다. 이 땅의 역사를 끌어안는

A Magnanimous Community of Love

Lee Kyungsoo (Literary Critic)

After publishing his first collection of poems, *"Jeon Bong-jun on his Way to Seoul,"* in 1985, then *"North Port"* in 2012, Ahn Do-Hyun stopped writing poetry for some years, but has recently begun again. The attitude penetrating his poetry can be considered as a gaze of love and solidarity directed at those who are marginalized. The poet's gaze reaches not only the world where humans live together but also the world of nature.

The poetry of Ahn Do-Hyun generally speaking includes the major theme of love, but the interesting thing is that he does not stop at the sense of personal

그의 관점과 남과 북을 아우르는 시선, 소외된 자리를 향한 따뜻한 연대의 태도는 그의 시가 민중시의 계보를 잇고 있음을 단적으로 보여준다. 여기에 서로 긴밀히 연결되어 있는 생명의 그물에 대한 생태학적 인식과 긍정의 시선, 모든 대상을 감싸 안는 사랑이라는 주제의 어울림이 안도현 시의 개성적 자리를 마련한다.

안도현의 시는 대부분 사랑의 노래라고 해도 과언이 아니다. 대상을 향한 사랑이나 그리움의 감정이 그의 시에는 지속적으로 나타난다. 흥미로운 것은 사랑을 노래한 연애시의 형식을 띠고 있는 시들에서조차 그의 시가 개인적 사랑의 감정을 노래하는 데 그치지 않는다는 것이다. 소외된 이들과 낮은 곳을 포괄하는 공동체적 사랑의 태도를 그의 시는 일관되게 보여준다.

「그대에게 가고 싶다」에서 "그대 보고 싶은 마음"은 "밤새 퍼부어대던 눈발"도 그치게 하고 "하늘도 맨 처음인 듯 열리"게 한다. 시의 화자가 생각하는 "사랑이란/또 다른 길을 찾아 두리번거리지 않고" "혼자서는 가지 않는 것"이다. "지치고 상처입고 구멍난 삶을 데리고/그대에게 가고 싶다"고 그가 말할 때 그가 꿈꾸는 사랑은 이미 개인적 사랑의 의미를 넘어선다. "우리가

love but extends to a wider love. This is closely related to the fact that his poetry is connected to the emotions of the "Minjung" poetry of the 1980s. His vision embracing the history of our land, his gaze encompassing the North and the South, and his warm attitude toward marginalized areas, show plainly that his poetry has inherited the genealogy of Minjung poetry. Hence, the ecological perception and affirmative regard for the network of life, and the resonance of the theme of the love that embraces all objects, provide the unique character of Ahn Do-Hyun's poetry.

It is no exaggeration to say that Ahn Do-Hyun's poems are mostly love songs. The emotions of love and yearning for the beloved appear constantly in his poems. What is interesting is that even in the poems which adopt the forms of love poetry, his poetry is not limited to singing about feelings of personal love. His poems consistently show attitudes of communal love, including those who are marginalized and low.

In *"I Long to Go toward You"*, the "heart longing to see you" stops "the snow that was driving down all night long" and "the sky opens as though for the first time." The poem's speaker thinks, "Love is a matter of

함께 만들어야 할 신천지/우리가 더불어 세워야 할 나라"에 대한 열망이 그대에게 가고 싶은 사랑과 그리움의 마음을 "무장무장" 타오르게 한다. 사랑하는 그대에게 보내는 유언 같은 시 「마지막 편지」에서도 안도현은 개인적 사랑의 한계에 갇히지 않는 사랑에 대해 노래한다. "이 세상을 나누어 껴안고" "괴로워하리라"는 다짐은 이 시에서 추구하는 진정한 사랑의 의미를 짐작케 한다. 사랑을 잃는다 해도 울지 말고 "길 잃은 아이처럼 서 있지 말고/그대가 길이 되어 가"라고 당부하는 비장한 태도는 결국 사랑의 마음조차 숨길 만큼 이 세상의 아픔과 슬픔이 크고, 가야 할 길이 멀다는 뜻이기도 하다. 「바닷가 우체국」처럼 그리움의 정서와 시간을 품은 소재가 등장할 때 안도현 시의 아름다움은 특히 빛을 발한다. "내가 이곳에 오기 아주 오래 전부터" "두 눈이 짓무르도록 수평선을 바라보았"고 "그리하여 귓속에 파도 소리가 모래처럼 쌓였을" 바닷가 우체국을 스쳐간 세월을 이해하는 순간, "나는 곧 그 게으름을 이해할 수 있었다"고 화자는 고백한다. 누군가를 그리워하고 사랑하는 일 또한 그런 것임을 이 시를 읽다 보면 자연스럽게 이해하게 된다. 「오래 된 우물」은 시적 대상을 바

not... taking another path," "of not advancing alone." When he says, "I long to go toward you, bringing a weary, wounded, threadbare life," the love that he dreams of already exceeds the meaning of personal love. The desire for "the new world we must create together, the nation we must establish together," makes the heart with its love that yearns to go toward you "fiercely blaze." In the poem *"Last Letter,"* a poem that sounds like a testament sent to the beloved, Ahn Do-Hyun again sings of a love that is not confined to the limits of personal love. The promise to "share up this world, each embracing a part, and suffering torment" hints at the real sense of the love being sought in this poem. Even if you lose your love, the pathetic attitude that insists "don't cry, I beg. Do not stand like a child that has lost its way. Become your own path and go," eventually suggests that the pain and sorrow of this world is so great that it hides even the heart of love, while the path ahead is long. When the topic of the emotions of yearning and time emerge as in the poem *"Seaside Post Office"* the beauty of Ahn Do-Hyun's poetry shines forth especially. "Long before I came here the post office had probably been gazing at the hori-

라보는 시인의 태도를 보여주는 일종의 알레고리 시인데, 여기서 생명을 지닌 존재이자 시간의 역사와 삶의 흔적을 품은 존재로 오래된 우물을 대하는 화자의 태도는 사랑하는 이를 대하는 태도와 별반 다르지 않다.

안도현의 시에서 지속적으로 발견되는 또 하나의 특징은 그가 여전히 자연을 시적 상상력의 원천으로 삼고 있는 시인이라는 점이다. 그의 시에는 자연과의 교감이 아름답게 그려져 있는데 이런 특징은 사실상 오늘날 우리 시가 점점 잃어 가고 있는 미덕이기도 하다. 안도현의 시는 따뜻하고 아름다운 자연 서정시가 지닌 미덕과 효과를 여실히 보여준다.

"세상에 나누어줄 것이 많다는 듯이" "한 잎 두 잎" "낮은 곳으로/자꾸 내려앉"는 가을 낙엽을 노래한 「가을 엽서」, "내게 땅이 있다면/거기에 나팔꽃을 심"어 "나팔꽃이 다 피었다 진 자리에/동그랗게 맺힌 꽃씨를 모아/아직 터지지 않은 세계를" 아들에게 물려주겠다고 노래한 「땅」, "허리를 낮출 줄 아는 사람에게만/보이는" 제비꽃과 사람 사이의 교감을 인상적으로 그린 「제비꽃에 대하여」, 붉은 명자꽃의 이미지로 각인되어 있는 명자 누나의 서글픈 삶을 붉은 색의 이미지를 활

zon until its eyes were sore, while the sound of waves must have piled up like sand in its ears" and as he understands the years that have passed by the beach post office, the speaker confesses that he "could understand that laziness." Anyone who reads this poem will understand naturally that there is such a thing as missing and loving someone. *"The Ancient Well"* is a kind of allegory that shows the attitude of the poet looking at a poetic object. It is a living being here, with a history in time and traces of life and the attitude of the speaker toward the old well is not unlike a person's attitude toward a loved one.

Another feature that is constantly found in Ahn Do-Hyun's poems is that he is ever a poet who makes nature a source of his poetic imagination. In his poems, sympathy with nature is beautifully depicted, a characteristic which is a virtue our poetry is losing more and more today. Ahn Do-Hyun's poetry shows the virtues and effects possessed by warm and beautiful nature-centered lyric poetry.

"There's plenty to share in life" "one by one, leaves" "keep falling, settling in lowly places": the poem *"Autumn Postcard"* sings about autumn leaves falling.

용해 그린 「명자꽃」, 자연이 주는 깨달음을 노래한 「간격」 등은 모두 자연에서 상상력을 길어 올린 시들이다.

「간격」에서 시의 화자는 숲을 멀리서 바라볼 때는 나무와 나무가 모여 어깨를 대고 서 있어야 숲을 이루는 줄 알았는데 막상 숲에 들어가 보니 "나무와 나무 사이/넓거나 좁은 간격이 있다는 걸" 알게 되었다고 고백한다. "나무와 나무 사이/그 간격과 간격이 모여/鬱鬱蒼蒼 숲을 이룬다는 것을/산불이 휩쓸고 지나간/숲에 들어가 보고서야 알았다"는 고백이 의미심장한 것은, 그것이 사실은 자연뿐만 아니라 인간관계에도 적용되는 섭리이기 때문일 것이다. 안도현의 시는 오랫동안 하나 됨을 노래해 왔지만 주체와 타자 간에 간격이 없는 하나 됨은 사실상 불가능한 것임을 이해하고 있다. 타자와의 간격을 유지하고 이 간격을 지나치게 침범하지 않으면서 타자를 존중해 줄 때 비로소 숲이라는 공동체는 가능해진다. 이처럼 자연으로부터 얻은 깨달음은 안도현 시의 상상력의 원천이 된다.

자연을 시적 상상력으로 삼는 시인에게서는 아이 같은 시선이 종종 모습을 드러낸다. 안도현은 어른을 위한 동화를 여러 편 쓰기도 했듯이, 여전히 동심을 간직

"Ground" sings "If I had some ground I would sow it with morning glories" and then, "after the flowers had bloomed and faded I would gather together the spherical seeds" and bequeath to his son "a world that has not yet opened." *"Concerning Violets"* is a striking poem about sympathy between people and flowers which "can only be seen by someone who knows how to bend down low." The poem *"Flowering Myeongja Quince Blossom"* employs the image of a red quince flower to evoke the sad life of young Myeong-ja. The poem *"Gaps"* sings of the discoveries offered by nature; it and many other poems draw their imagination from nature.

When the speaker of the poem "Gaps" sees a forest from a distance he says, "I thought that one tree after another had gathered together, shoulder to shoulder, and formed a forest. But after entering the forest he realizes "that between one tree and another there is a gap, wide or narrow." He confesses that "one tree must stand well apart from the next, for it's the gaps between them gathered together that compose a leafy, green forest. I only realized that after I went into the forest and looked after a fire had swept through it."

하고 있는 시인이다. 그의 시에 자연의 인과관계를 뒤집어 보는 발상이나 가정법의 수사가 종종 등장하는 이유도 이와 무관해 보이지 않는다.

"이 세상에 아이들이 없다면"이라는 가정으로 시작된 시 「이 세상에 아이들이 없다면」은 그로 인해 역시 없을 것들로 어른들, 교육, 교과서, 시험, 대학교, 고등학교, 중학교, 국민학교, 운동장, 미끄럼틀을 나열하다가 마침내 "미끄럼틀을 타고/매일 매일 하늘에서 내려오는/눈부신 하느님을 본 사람은 아무도 없을 것이다"라는 문장으로 시가 마무리된다. 결국 이 시에서 아이는 '눈부신 하느님'과 동격이 된다.

마지막으로 하나 더 눈여겨볼 만한 특징은 그의 시에 하나 됨의 상상력, 즉 통일 지향의 세계관이 드러나고 있다는 점이다. 「청진 여자」는 남과 북을 하나로 연결하는 통일 지향적 상상력을 보여주는 대표적인 예이다. 통일과 자주의 이념을 청진 여자와의 간섭받지 않는 하룻밤 사랑에 빗댄 이 시의 상상력은 사실상 1980년대 민중시에서 익숙하게 보아오던 상상력이다. 지금은 시대착오적이고 남성 중심적인 시선으로 느껴지는 것이 사실이지만 그것은 이 시가 남과 북의 하나 됨이라는

The discovery applies not only to nature but also to human relations. Ahn Do-Hyun's poems have long been singing about unity, but he understands that it is virtually impossible for there to be a unity without gaps between one subject and another. The community of the forest only becomes possible when we preserve the gaps between us and others and respect the other without excessively intruding on this gap. Such enlightenment from nature is the source of the imagination of Ahn Do-Hyun.

In poets who find in nature a poetic imagination, a childlike way of seeing is often found. Ahn Do-Hyun is a poet who still keeps a childish innocence, just as he has written several fairy tales for adults. The reason why his poetry often turns out to be an investigation of an idea or assumption that overturns the cause-and-effect relationship of nature does not seem to be unrelated to that.

The poem *"If There Were no Children in this World"* starts by assuming that there are no children, and goes on to list all the other things that would also not exist: adults, education, textbooks, examinations, universities, high schools, middle schools, elementary schools, play-

통일과 자주의 이념을 사랑의 알레고리를 통해 표현했기 때문이다.

사실 안도현의 시에서는 위에서 언급한 네 가지 특징이 둘 이상씩 결합해 동시에 드러나는 경우가 대부분이다. 앞에서 살펴본 시들 외에도 「우리가 눈발이라면」, 「고래를 기다리며」 같은 시가 대표적이다. 「우리가 눈발이라면」에서 "사람이 사는 마을/가장 낮은 곳으로/따뜻한 함박눈이 되어 내리자", "그이의 깊고 붉은 상처 위에 돋는/새 살이 되자"고 말할 때 눈은 가장 낮은 곳의 아픔과 추위를 보듬고 상처를 치유하며 내린다. 안도현의 시에서 자연은 이와 같이 정서를 품은 대상이자 춥고 소외되고 낮고 아픈 곳을 보듬어 안는 치유의 상상력을 지닌 존재로 그려진다. 「고래를 기다리며」에는 "기다리는 것은 오지 않는다는 것을/알면서도 기다리고, 기다리다 지치는 게 삶이라고/알면서도" 고래를 기다리는 화자가 등장한다. 이 하염없는 기다림은 마침내 "숨을 한 번 내쉴 때마다/어깨를 들썩이는 그 바다"에서 "한 마리 고래"를 보아내기에 이른다. 간절한 기다림이 불러온 고래인 셈이다.

안도현의 시가 그려낸 웅숭깊은 사랑의 노래는 역사

grounds and slides, The poem ends: "There would be nobody who ever saw how, dazzling, God comes sliding down from heaven every day." At the end of this poem, the child is identified with a "dazzling god."

Finally, one more remarkable feature is the imagination of becoming one in his poetry, that is, the way a unified worldview is revealed. *"Woman of Cheongjin"* is a typical example of a unification-oriented imagination that connects North and South. The imagination of an idea of unity and autonomy alluded to in this poem as an unimpeded one-night-stand with the woman of Cheongjin is in fact an imagination familiar from the Minjung poetry of the 1980s. Today it seems to be an anachronistic and male-centered way of looking, but it is because this poem expresses an idea of unification and autonomy, North and South becoming one, through an allegory of love.

In actual fact, in the poems of Ahn Do-Hyun, two or more of the above mentioned four features are usually combined and revealed at the same time. In addition to the poems already mentioned, poems like *"If We Are Falling Snow"* and *"Waiting for Whales"* are significant. When *"If We Are Falling Snow"* says, "let us turn

의 시간과 소외된 이들을 품고 사랑과 생명의 공동체를 구축해 가고 있다. 자연으로부터 얻은 상상력을 바탕으로 위계 없이 나란한 존재들이 더불어 살아가는 공동체를 그의 시가 그려갈 수 있기를 기대해 본다.

into thick, warm snowflakes and fall on the lowest places in villages where people live," or "become new flesh covering that person's deep, crimson wounds" it shows snow falling and embracing what is low and cold, healing wounds. In these poems, nature is portrayed as a person with emotions, a being with an imagination of healing that embraces cold, marginalized, low and sick places. In *"Waiting for Whales,"* the speaker says, "Though I knew that what we wait for never comes, I waited; though I knew that life is a matter of growing weary of waiting." This endless waiting finally leads to the appearance of a "whale" in "the sea with its shoulders heaving every time it took a breath". It is a whale that is summoned by an eager waiting.

The magnanimous love song represented by the poems of Ahn Do-Hyun continues to build a community of love and life with the time of history and alienated people. Based on an imagination received from nature, his poetry hopes to be able to depict a community where beings live together in equality without hierarchy.

안도현에
대해

What They Say
About Ahn Do-Hyun

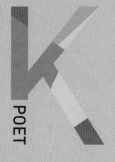

POET

안도현 시인은 1970년대 후반부터 시를 쓰기 시작하여 80, 90년대를 거치며 왕성하게 시작활동을 해왔고 지금도 한국시단의 중심에 위치해 있다.

일본어로 출간된 그의 시집을 읽고서 큰 감명을 받았다. 가슴을 울리는 시들로 가득했다. 동시대를 사는 시인으로서 어떻게 이처럼 폭넓은 감성과 깊은 사유를 가졌는지 충격을 받을 만큼 좋은 시들로 가득했다. 그와 나는 나라는 다르지만 둘 다 청년기에 고도 경제성장을 경험했으며, 그 후 큰 의미에서의 정치적 모순을 공

The poet Ahn Do-Hyun began to write poetry in the late 1970s, was active throughout the 80s and 90s, and still today stands at the center of Korea's community of poets.

I was much impressed on reading a volume of his poems published in Japanese. It was filled with poems that made my heart ring. It was filled with fine poems that left me wondering how, as a poet of contemporary life, he was capable of such wide sensitivity and deep thought. He and I, though we are from different nations, both experienced high economic growth in

유한다. 그 정치적 모순은 80, 90년대 이후, 국가의 틀을 넘어 인간의 존재와 관련된 문제로 전환되어갔던 것이다. 그것은 우리에게 닫힌 사고로부터 열린 사고로의 발상 전환을 촉구했다. 그의 작품들에 이런 문제가 공유되어 있어 더욱 흥미로웠다.

안도현의 시는 생활자로부터 결코 눈을 돌리지 않는다. 예술이나 문학이 사람의 생활로부터 괴리되는 것을 철저히 거부하고 있다. 이는 한국의 시가 전통적으로 소중히 여겨왔던 점이기도 할 것이다. 근래에는 한국에서도 포스트모더니즘의 영향을 받은, 다양한 실험적 작품이 태어나고 있는 것 같다. 그러나 그의 시는 그런 시들과 선 하나를 그어놓고, 시의 주류는 민중의 마음과 함께 있다. 한국이 현재도 계속해서 시의 나라로 남아있는 이유가 거기 있다고 생각한다.

안도현은 서정이라는 국자로 현실로부터 시를 퍼 올리는 시인이다. 그 국자는 철학적 사색이라는 윤곽을 가지고 있다. 국자의 무늬는 잘 닦여진, 칠하지 않은 나무 같은 그의 팔이며 거기로 흐르는 피는 따스함을 가진 사랑이다. 한 사람의 여성을 사랑하듯 그는 언어를

our youth, and then shared political contradictions in the wider sense. Those political contradictions shifted after the 1980s and 1990s to problems related to human existence going beyond the limits of the nation. That urged us to switch from a closed way of thinking to an open way of thinking. His work was all the more interesting because it shared these problems.

Ahn Do-Hyun's poems never turn their eyes away from living beings. He firmly refuses to separate art and literature from human life. This is something that Korean poetry has traditionally regarded as important. In recent years, various experimental works influenced by postmodernism seem to have appeared in Korea. However, his poetry stands apart from such poems and the mainstream of his poems is with the hearts of the people. I think that is the reason why Korea still today remains a land of poetry.

Ahn Do-Hyun is a poet who uses the ladle of lyricism to scoop poetry from reality. That ladle has contours of philosophical thought. The pattern of the ladle is a love with the warmth of his arm, like well-

사랑하고 있다. 그의 팔은 물 위로 석양빛이 떨어지는 수평선 주변으로, 수목의 줄기 속으로, 석탄 스토브의 작열하는 불 속으로 부드럽게 퍼져 나간다. 그리고 욕심 부리지 않고 손에 담을 만큼의 시만을 퍼온다. 어느 작품에도 호들갑스러움이 느껴지지 않고 비유 하나하나가 매끄러운 것은 그 때문이다. 언어는 시인의 육체 속에 있고 기쁨 속에 있다.

그는 사랑하는 사람을 향해 끝나지 않을 편지를 쓰듯이 그렇게 시를 써왔고 앞으로도 써나갈 것이라고 생각한다.

시바타 산키치(일본)

시인이 '보는 사람'이라면 안도현은 "세상의 뒤쪽이거나 아래쪽"을 보아내는 것으로는 이미 일가를 이루었다. 그가 보아내는 존재들은 사람이기도 하고 자연이기도 하며 무엇보다 우리가 우리 뒤로 미뤄놓았던 감정의 본모습이기도 하다. 그것들은 한없이 연약해서 안도현은 언어의 손길로 가만가만 어루만진다. 그 사소하지만 소중한 것들을 어루만지고 감싸 안으면서 안도현의 시

worn, unvarnished wood, and the blood that flows into it. He loves language as one might love a woman. His arms reach out gently toward a horizon where the sun is setting over the water, toward the trunks of trees, the fire blazing in a coal stove. And he is not greedy, he only scoops out enough for his hands to hold. That is why one does not feel agitation in any of his works, and therefore the images flow smoothly. Language is inside the poet's body and in his joy.

He has for long written poetry like an unending letter to a loved one, and I think he will continue to write in that way. Shibata Sankichi.

Shibata Sankichi(Japan)

If the poet is a 'seeer', Ahn Do-Hyun has already established his reputation by seeing "the back or the bottom of the world". The beings he sees may be people or nature, but above all, they are the true likeness of emotions that we have thrust behind us. They are infinitely fragile, so Ahn Do-Hyun caresses them very lightly with a touch of language. As he touches

는 우리 세계의 거대한 사랑 하나를 기어이 완성해내려
는 중이다.

김 근

　나는 1990년대 초부터 일본에 한국시를 번역 소개해
왔는데, 안도현 시인이 한국 전후세대 시인 중 가장 사
랑을 받는다고 단언할 수 있다. 그는 한국 전후세대 시
인 최초로 일본의 출판사에서 시집 출판 제의를 받았
다. 이 시집이 견인차 역할을 해주어 지금은 수많은 한
국시를 일본어 시집으로 번역 출간하고 있다. 나에게도
일본어 시집 번역은 처음이었는데 가장 행복한 기억으
로 남아 있다.
　일본의 미디어도 크게 관심을 가져, 니시니혼 신문에
서는 안도현 시인에게 3개월간 매일 게재하는 방식의
에세이 연재 원고청탁을 해왔다. 이 연재는 엄청난 반
향을 일으켰고 책으로 묶여 일본에서 출판되기도 했다.
　일본의 한 젊은 시인은 책상 앞에 안도현의 시를 붙여
놓고 늘 읽고 있다고 했다. 현재도 일본 최고의 인터넷
사이트에서 수많은 독자들이 안도현의 시로 자신의 블

and embraces those little but precious things, Ahn Do-Hyun's poems aim to achieve a huge love of our world.

Kim Keun

I have been translating and introducing Korean poetry to Japan since the early 1990s, and I can affirm that poet Ahn Do-Hyun is the most beloved poet of Korea's postwar generations. He was the first poet of the Korean postwar era to receive an offer to publish a collection from a Japanese publishing house. That collection served as a driving force and now many Korean poems are translated and published in Japanese. It was my first time to translate a poetry collection into Japanese, and it remains my happiest memory.

The Japanese media have been very interested, and the *Nishinihon Shimbun* asked the poet Ahn Do-Hyun to contribute an essay series every day for three months. This series made a tremendous impact and has been published in Japan in book form.

A young Japanese poet has told how he has fixed

로그를 장식하고 있다.

한성례

나는 안도현 시인이 '연탄'을 소재로 한 시를 좋아한다. 아무도 거들떠보지 않는 연탄에도 사랑을 줄 줄 아는 시인의 시. 「가을 엽서」에서도 낮은 곳으로 자꾸 내려앉는 낙엽은 가을이 되어 그냥 떨어지는 낙엽이 아니라 땅에 사랑을 주려고 살포시 내려앉는다는 것을 배운다. 나의 인생관인 낙관주의를 안도현의 시에서 찾아볼 수 있어서 세계 사람들에게 모든 걸 긍정적으로 받아드려야 한다는 것을 알릴 수 있다.

괵셀 튀르쾨쥬(터키)

그의 작품 중 가장 잘 알려진 『연어』처럼 안도현의 시는 반짝거리며 흐른다. 사람과의 교제의 귀중함을 무감각하게 위협하는 일상생활의 압박감 속에서, 그의 「겨울 강가에서」 「연탄 한 장」 시들에 나타나는 기품과 겸손함은 우리의 삶을 지속시켜 주는 건 서로와의 훈훈함과 기본적 품위라는 것을 편안히 상기시킨다. 우리는

one of Ahn Do-Hyun's poems in front of his desk and reads it all the time. Many readers are still decorating their blogs with Ahn Do-Hyun's poems in Japan's best internet sites.

Han Sung Rea

I like Ahn Do-Hyun's poem 'A Coal Briquette.' It's a poem by a poet who knows how to give love to a briquette that everyone despises. In *"An Autumn Postcard"* we learn that the leaves that keep falling to the lowest place once autumn comes are not just leaves falling, but they are falling gently in order to give love to the ground. You can find the optimism that is my view of life in Ahn Do-Hyun's poems, so I can tell the world's inhabitants that they should accept everything positively.

Göksel Türközü(Turkey)

Ahn Do-Hyun's poetry glistens and flows like the salmon of his well-known novel *"The Salmon Who Dared to Leap Higher."* The grace and humility appearing in poems such as *"On a Winter River Bank"*

안도현의 시적세계에서 삶을 살만한 가치가 있게 하는
작은 기쁨을 발견할 수 있다.

브루스 풀턴(미국)

and *"One Coal Briquette"* are a comforting reminder of the warmth and decency that sustain our lives at a time when the pressures of daily life threaten to numb us to the value of human companionship. In Ahn Do-Hyun's poetic world we can discover the small pleasures that make life worth living.

Bruce Fulton(USA)

K-포엣
안도현 시선

2017년 10월 10일 초판 1쇄 발행
2024년 7월 29일 초판 2쇄 발행

지은이 안도현 | **옮긴이** 안선재 | **펴낸이** 김재범
펴낸곳 (주)아시아 | **출판등록** 2006년 1월 27일 제406-2006-000004호
주소 경기도 파주시 회동길 445(서울 사무소: 서울특별시 동작구 서달로 161-1 3층)
홈페이지 www.bookasia.org
전자우편 bookasia@hanmail.net
ISBN 979-11-5662-317-5 (set) | 979-11-5662-320-5 (04810)
값은 뒤표지에 있습니다.

K-Poet
Poems by Ahn Do-Hyun

Written by Ahn Do-Hyun | **Translated by** Brother Anthony of Taizé
Published by ASIA Publishers
Address 445, Hoedong-gil, Paju-si, Gyeonggi-do, Korea
(Seoul Office: 161-1, Seodal-ro, Dongjak-gu, Seoul, Korea)
Homepage Address www.bookasia.org
E-mail bookasia@hanmail.net
ISBN 979-11-5662-317-5 (set) | 979-11-5662-320-5 (04810)
First published in Korea by ASIA Publishers 2017

This book is published with the support of the Literature Translation Institute of Korea
(LTI Korea).